And when it was time,
came a teeny-tiny cree
She was all alone.

The creepy-crawly bug held up her
head, looked out at the beautiful
meadow, and said, "I don't know much,
but I know what I know. I gotta go!
I gotta go! I gotta go to Mexico!"

And she creepy-crawled away just as fast as she could go.

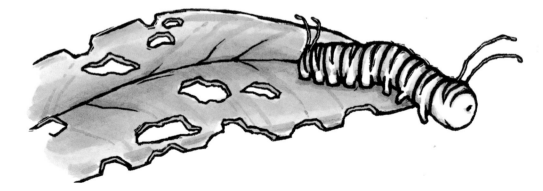

She ate and she crawled. She crawled
and she ate.

She ate so much she crawled
right out of her skin. "I gotta go!
I gotta go! I gotta go to Mexico!"

Along the way, she met a grasshopper
who said, "Where are you going, creepy-
crawly bug?"

"Mexico! Mexico! I gotta go to Mexico!"

"Mexico?" said the grasshopper. "What
on earth is Mexico?"

"I have no idea," said the creepy-crawly
bug. "But if Mexico is where I'm going,
and it is, then Mexico will be wherever
I get."

And she creepy-crawled away just as fast
as she could go.

Next she met an ant who said, "Where are you going, creepy-crawly bug?"

"Mexico! Mexico! I gotta go to Mexico!"

"Mexico?" said the ant. "Never heard of it. How will you get to Mexico?"

"I have no idea," said the creepy-crawly bug. "But if Mexico is where I'm going, and it is, then however I go, I will get there."

And she creepy-crawled away just as fast as she could go.

After she had creepy-crawled a very long time, the creepy-crawly bug was still in the beautiful meadow and Mexico was nowhere in sight. "Oh, my, my, my, my, my," she sighed. "Knowing what you know is sometimes very hard." She was so tired she couldn't creepy-crawl another inch. So she made herself a bed, tucked herself in tight, and said, "After a nice long rest I'm sure I'll feel like a brand-new creepy-crawly bug."

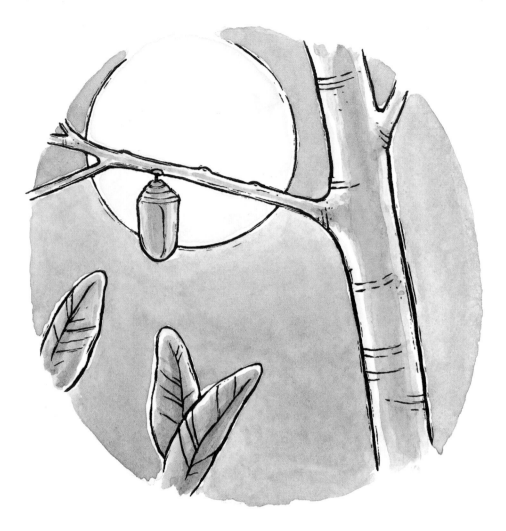

For days she slept, and days, hidden from
the world. Her sleep was long and hard
and very strange.

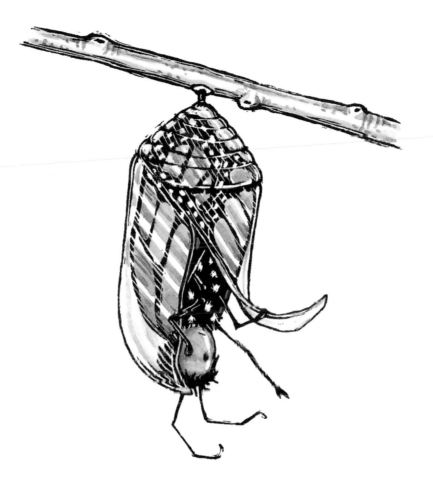

When it was time, she woke. She woke
and found she was indeed a brand-new
creepy-crawly bug.

She was a brand-new creepy-crawly bug
with wings. They were orange and black
and splendid.
She lifted her head, looked out at the
beautiful meadow, and said, "I gotta go!
I gotta go! I gotta go to Mexico!"
And off she flew just as fast as she
could go.

Along the way, she met a bird who said,
"Where are you going, creepy-crawly
bug with wings?"
"Mexico! Mexico! I gotta go to Mexico!"
"Mexico is thousands of miles from here!
A teeny-tiny bug like you will never
make it!"

But the creepy-crawly bug said, "I am
what I am and I know what I know, and
make it or not, I gotta go! I gotta go!
I gotta go to Mexico!"
And off she flew just as fast as she
could go.

She flew over farms and highways, cities and towns, forests and rivers. For days she flew, and days, all on her own and only knowing what she knew, but still she flew and still she cried, "Mexico! Mexico! I gotta go to Mexico!"

Her journey was long and hard and full of dangers.

At last she came to a valley. Far below
she saw millions of bugs just like her.
They covered the trees, changing the
green to orange. She drifted down
and joined them. All but one was
fast asleep.

"Hello," she said.

"Hello," he said. "Welcome to Mexico."

"I am so glad to be here," she said,
and she fell asleep.

Winter came. The creepy-crawly bugs
slept and slept.

In spring, the sun woke them.

"Good morning."

"Good morning."

"Will you dance with me?"

"Why, yes, thank you. I'd love to."

Two by two the creepy-crawly bugs flew

into the sky and danced, changing the

blue to orange.

When the dance was done, the creepy-crawly bug turned her head, looked toward home, and said, "I gotta go! I gotta go!"

"Goodbye!"

"Goodbye!"

Again she flew. She flew over rivers and forests, towns and cities, highways and farms. For days she flew, and days, all on her own and only knowing what she knew.

At last she came to a meadow.
She fluttered for a while, looking
for the one leaf that would do, and,
landing lightly, laid the first of many
eggs. It was the reason for everything.

And when it was time, out of the egg
came a teeny-tiny creepy-crawly bug.